KU-655-970

EPISODE VI
RETURN OF THE JEDI

RYDER WINDHAM

BASED ON THE STORY BY
GEORGE LUCAS

AND THE SCREENPLAY BY
LAWRENCE KASDAN

ILLUSTRATIONS BY
BRIAN ROOD

EGMONT

We bring stories to life

First published in Great Britain 2016 by Egmont UK Limited
The Yellow Building, 1 Nicholas Road, London W11 4AN

Written by Ryder Windham
Covers and Tin Design by Maddox Philpot
Illustrated by Brian Rood

© & ™ 2016 Lucasfilm Ltd.
ISBN 978 1 4052 8285 7
63690/1
Printed in China

To find more great *Star Wars* books, visit www.egmont.co.uk/starwars

All rights reserved. No part of this book may be reproduced, stored in a retrieval system, or transmitted, in any form or by any means, electronic, mechanical, photocopying, recording or otherwise, without written permission of the publisher and copyright holders.

Stay safe online. Any website addresses listed in this book are correct at the time of going to print. However, Egmont is not responsible for content hosted by third parties. Please be aware that online content can be subject to change and websites can contain content that is unsuitable for children. We advise that all children are supervised when using the internet.

A LONG TIME AGO IN A GALAXY FAR, FAR AWAY ....

LUKE SKYWALKER HAS RETURNED to his home planet of Tatooine in an attempt to rescue his friend Han Solo from the clutches of the vile gangster Jabba the Hutt.

Little does Luke know that the Galactic Empire has secretly begun construction on a new armoured space station even more powerful than the first dreaded Death Star.

When completed, this ultimate weapon will spell certain doom for the small band of rebels struggling to restore freedom to the galaxy ...

THE SECOND Death Star was far from finished. An Imperial Star Destroyer arrived near the building site; then a shuttle and two TIE fighters dropped out of the Star Destroyer's main hangar. As the shuttle and its escorts travelled towards the Death Star, its captain spoke into a comlink: 'Command station, we're starting our approach. Deactivate the security shield.'

On the shuttle, Darth Vader peered through a window at the monstrous space station. He was thinking about his son, Luke Skywalker ... and how he could convert him to the dark side.

THE DEATH STAR'S commanding officer, Moff Jerjerrod, greeted Darth Vader.

'Lord Vader,' Jerjerrod said. 'This is an unexpected pleasure. We're honoured by your presence.'

'You may dispense with the pleasantries, Commander,' Vader said, not breaking his stride as he moved past the gathered troops. 'I'm here to put you back on schedule.'

'I tell you, this station will be operational as planned.'

Turning to face Jerjerrod, Vader said, 'The Emperor is most displeased with your apparent lack of progress.'

Jerjerrod looked nervous. 'We shall double our efforts,' he said.

'I hope so, Commander, for your sake. The Emperor is not as forgiving as I am.'

Vader turned and walked out of the hangar, leaving Jerjerrod to prepare for the Emperor's arrival.

ON TATOOINE, C-3PO and R2-D2 were making their way up a hill to Jabba the Hutt's palace. They were part of a plan to rescue Han Solo, who had been frozen in carbonite and delivered to Jabba by a bounty hunter named Boba Fett.

'Of course I'm worried,' the protocol droid said. 'Lando Calrissian and poor Chewbacca never returned from this awful place.'

C-3PO hesitantly approached the gigantic door and knocked. Suddenly, there was a metallic grinding noise and the door began to rise. The door was still opening as R2-D2 scooted under it and into the citadel's dark, cavernous entry.

'Artoo, wait,' C-3PO called. 'Oh, dear!'

JABBA'S THRONE ROOM was a dimly lit chamber that was crawling with grotesque creatures. Jabba himself rested his bulky form on a broad dais.

C-3PO bowed and said, 'Good morning.'

R2-D2 rotated his dome and projected his holographic message of Luke Skywalker, who said: 'Greetings, Exalted One. I am Luke Skywalker, Jedi Knight and friend to Captain Solo. I seek an audience with Your Greatness to bargain for Solo's life.'

Hearing this, Jabba laughed heartily.

Luke's hologram continued. 'As a token of my goodwill, I present to you a gift: these two droids.'

Hearing this, C-3PO muttered, 'We're doomed.'

JABBA WAS HAVING A PARTY.

Female aliens danced to the rhythms of the Max Rebo Band. On the bandstand, Max Rebo – a blue-skinned Ortolan – performed the music. While the music played, a Twi'lek named Oola danced, too.

Jabba asked Oola to come sit with him. When she refused, Jabba slammed his fist down on a button. A trapdoor opened beneath her and Oola plummeted through the floor.

While Jabba's friends looked down through the grating to watch Oola meet her doom, C-3PO shook his head and turned away. He glanced at the carbonite form of Han Solo, which was hanging on the wall, and wondered if he'd ever leave Jabba's palace in one piece.

LATER, TWO MYSTERIOUS FIGURES entered the throne room: a bounty hunter named Boushh held a leash that led to the neck of the second figure, a tall, furry Wookiee.

On his dais, Jabba grinned and said, 'At last we have the mighty Chewbacca.'

Speaking through C-3PO to translate, Boushh said, 'I want fifty thousand. No less.'

Jabba flew into a rage. C-3PO spoke for Jabba: 'The mighty Jabba asks why he must pay fifty thousand.'

Boushh's left hand revealed a metal orb.

Cringing, C-3PO cried out, 'Because he's holding a thermal detonator!'

Jabba began to laugh. 'This bounty hunter is my kind of scum … fearless and inventive.'

A pair of Gamorrean guards grabbed Chewbacca and hauled him out of the room.

NIGHT FELL ON TATOOINE. Boushh stepped silently through the throne room. The bounty hunter looked up at where Han Solo hung on the wall, frozen in carbonite. Boushh pressed a button and then watched bright energy spill out of the carbon shell. The carbonite melted, and Han fell forward, collapsing on the sandy floor.

Boushh knelt beside him.

'I can't see,' Han said.

'Your eyesight will return in time,' Boushh replied.

Han shook. 'Who are you?'

Boushh removed his leather-and-metal helmet – it was Princess Leia! She said, 'Someone who loves you.'

'Leia!'

But then they both heard a low, rumbling laugh. A curtain slid back behind them to reveal Jabba the Hutt and his chortling minions. They were trapped!

ONCE AGAIN, there was silence in Jabba's throne room. Leia, eyes closed, sat beside Jabba's slumbering form. She had replaced Oola as Jabba's slave dancer.

Jabba's servant Bib Fortuna was also awake. Hearing the sound of footsteps descending the stairway from the main entrance, he saw Luke coming down. He told Luke to leave immediately.

Luke simply said, 'I must speak with Jabba.'

Hearing those words, Leia opened her eyes and sat up. *Luke!*

Luke stared hard at Bib and said, 'You will take me to Jabba now!'

Bib did not realise that Luke was using the Force to influence his thoughts.

He let Luke approach the dais. From behind Jabba, C-3PO cried out, 'At last! Master Luke's come to rescue me!'

JABBA'S HEAVY EYELIDS slid back and he let out a wet snort. 'You weak-minded fool!' Jabba said, scowling at Bib. 'He's using an old Jedi mind trick.'

Luke spotted the disguised Lando among Jabba's guards. Staring hard at Jabba, he said, 'You will bring Captain Solo and the Wookiee to me.'

Jabba laughed. 'Your mind powers will not work on me, boy.'

C-3PO saw that Luke was standing on the trapdoor. 'Master Luke,' the droid called out, 'you're – '

But Jabba interrupted: 'I shall enjoy watching you die.'

A guard's blaster suddenly jumped out of its holster and flew into Luke's waiting hand. As Luke raised the blaster, Jabba triggered the trapdoor – and both Luke and a Gamorrean guard plunged into the pit!

LUKE LANDED in a pile of skeletons. A horrific growl echoed from a cave beyond the door. The Gamorrean started squealing. From above, C-3PO cried out, 'Oh, no! The rancor!'

Lurching into the pit on two powerful legs, the rancor had an enormous fanged mouth. The guard tried to run away, but the rancor gobbled him up – and then turned for Luke.

The rancor swiped at him, but Luke dodged and ran for the cave. He picked up a skull from the cave floor and hurled it. The rancor was just ducking its head through the doorway when the skull smashed against the control panel. The heavy iron door crashed down on the rancor. The rancor was dead.

JABBA WAS ENRAGED and sentenced Luke and his friends to be fed to the Sarlacc, which lived in a pit in the desert. Not long afterward, a skiff flew over the desert. It was loaded with Jabba's guards – including Lando in disguise – and three bound captives: Luke, Han and Chewbacca. Leia was a prisoner in Jabba's sail barge, which flew next to the skiff.

When they arrived, at Jabba's command C-3PO picked up a comlink and announced, 'Victims of the almighty Sarlacc: should any of you wish to beg for mercy, the great Jabba the Hutt will now listen to your pleas.'

'Jabba!' Luke called out. 'This is your last chance. Free us or die.'

Jabba and his cronies were almost overcome by their own mocking laughter.

A GUARD PRODDED LUKE to the edge of the plank directly above the Sarlacc's gaping maw. Luke looked at R2-D2 on the barge's deck and gave him a signal. Luke then bounced off the plank skyward. R2-D2 simultaneously launched a lightsaber from his dome. Luke landed on the skiff and caught his lightsaber. He instantly ignited it and began to battle!

The Wookiee barked anxiously as Lando was knocked over the side of the skiff. Boba Fett, who was on the barge, fired the jets on his backpack and blasted away.

As Chewbacca untied Han's bonds, Fett landed on the prisoners' skiff and brought up his blaster rifle. He was going to shoot Luke!

BEFORE FETT COULD FIRE,

Luke spun with his lightsaber and hacked off the blaster's barrel. Chewbacca barked at Han.

'Boba Fett! Where?' Han answered. He was holding a spear that Chewbacca had directed him to pick up from the floor of the skiff, but he still couldn't see.

He turned blindly, swinging the spear hard. By sheer luck, it hit the bounty hunter's backpack. Fett was launched from the skiff like a missile. He bounced off the side of the sail barge and tumbled into the Sarlacc's mouth. A moment later, the Sarlacc burped loudly.

Meanwhile, on the sail barge, Leia leaped up behind Jabba, draping her chain over his head and around his neck. She pulled and pulled. A few moments later Jabba was dead.

BECAUSE JABBA'S GUARDS

were still firing a huge cannon at Luke's friends, Luke leaped from the skiff to the side of the sail barge. The gunners were about to release another barrage when Luke leaped onto the barge's deck. He activated his lightsaber and made quick work of them, then moved towards the other guards, cutting down their weapons and deflecting laser bolts back at the shooters.

During all the commotion, R2-D2 had managed to avoid being trampled and had returned to Jabba's banquet room to find Leia still chained to Jabba. R2-D2 extended his laser torch and fired a controlled burst at the chain, neatly cutting it in two and freeing Leia.

'Come on,' Leia said. 'We gotta get out of here.'

C-3PO HURRIED AFTER R2-D2, heading for the deck. Leia was already there, and she saw Luke fighting several guards. He caught sight of Leia and said, 'Get the gun!'

Leia ran to the large laser cannon and climbed onto the weapon's turret platform. As she began to swivel the cannon around, Luke raised his lightsaber to fend off another attacker and yelled, 'Point it at the deck!'

Luke ran to her. He took hold of a rope, then kicked the trigger of the laser cannon. The cannon fired into the deck as Luke and Leia swung to the skiff, joining Han, Chewie and Lando.

ON THE SKIFF, Luke said, 'Let's go! And don't forget the droids.'

Lando guided the skiff until they saw C-3PO's legs sticking out of the sand. Two large electromagnets hoisted both droids up just before a great explosion tore through the barge. A chain of explosions followed as Jabba's sail barge collapsed in a fiery blaze.

Soon afterward, Luke was alone piloting his X-wing, and Han and the others were on board the *Falcon*. After leaving Tatooine behind, the two ships veered off in different directions.

'Meet you back at the fleet,' Luke said into his helmet's comlink.

Han responded, 'Hey, Luke, thanks for coming after me.'

Luke smiled, then angled his ship for a distant star – Dagobah.

IN A GREAT DISPLAY of the Empire's might, thousands of TIE fighters orbited the Death Star to mark the arrival of Emperor Palpatine. Vader stood in a large docking bay and watched the Emperor's shuttle as it landed. The docking bay was filled nearly to capacity with Imperial troops in tight formation.

The landing ramp descended and Vader watched six members of the Royal Guard disembark. After the Royal Guard took their positions at the base of the landing ramp, the Emperor emerged. Darth Vader kneeled.

Hunched and walking with a gnarled cane, Emperor Palpatine had ghastly, withered features barely visible under the hood of his heavy black cloak. Stopping before Vader, the Emperor said, 'Rise, my friend.'

VADER ROSE TO WALK alongside the Emperor, who moved slowly past the long rows of troops.

'The Death Star will be completed on schedule,' Vader reported.

'You have done well, Lord Vader,' the Emperor replied, his voice a decrepit rasp. 'And now I sense you wish to continue your search for young Skywalker.'

'Yes, my master.'

'Patience, my friend. In time, he will seek you out. And when he does, you must bring him before *me*. He has grown *strong*. Only together can we turn him to the dark side of the Force.'

Vader said, 'As you wish.'

The Emperor said, 'Everything is proceeding as I have foreseen.' He cackled to himself, and the evil sound echoed across the docking bay.

'YOU HAVE DONE WELL,
LORD VADER.'

'THAT IS THE
WAY OF THINGS ...
THE WAY OF THE FORCE.'

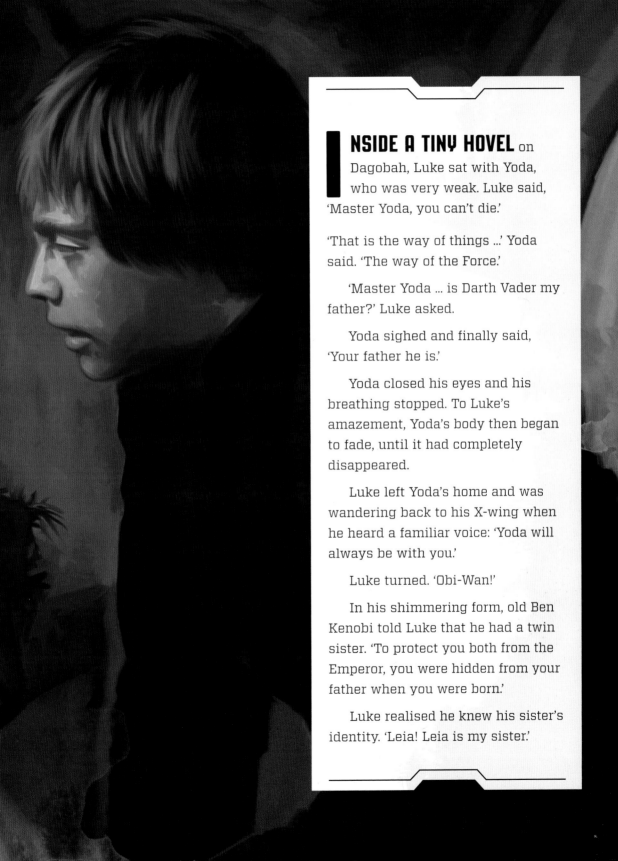

INSIDE A TINY HOVEL on Dagobah, Luke sat with Yoda, who was very weak. Luke said, 'Master Yoda, you can't die.'

'That is the way of things ...' Yoda said. 'The way of the Force.'

'Master Yoda ... is Darth Vader my father?' Luke asked.

Yoda sighed and finally said, 'Your father he is.'

Yoda closed his eyes and his breathing stopped. To Luke's amazement, Yoda's body then began to fade, until it had completely disappeared.

Luke left Yoda's home and was wandering back to his X-wing when he heard a familiar voice: 'Yoda will always be with you.'

Luke turned. 'Obi-Wan!'

In his shimmering form, old Ben Kenobi told Luke that he had a twin sister. 'To protect you both from the Emperor, you were hidden from your father when you were born.'

Luke realised he knew his sister's identity. 'Leia! Leia is my sister.'

ABOARD THE REBEL **ALLIANCE** flagship, Luke was reunited with all his friends. Mon Mothma, leader of the Rebellion, spoke to the assembled rebels: 'The time for our attack has come.'

Holograms of the Death Star and a green orb appeared.

'We also know that the weapon systems of this Death Star are not yet operational,' Mon Mothma added.

But the Death Star was protected by a shield projected from the nearby forest moon. 'A strike team will land on the moon and deactivate the shield generator,' said General Madine.

Then the rebel fleet would blow up the Death Star.

Han, Chewie, Luke and Leia volunteered to deactivate the shield generator on the forest moon. Lando would pilot the *Falcon* against the Death Star.

R2-D2 beeped a singsong observation.

C-3PO shuddered and replied, '"Exciting" is hardly the word I would choose.'

HAN SAT BEHIND the controls of the stolen Imperial shuttle as his friends looked on nervously. Their shuttle dropped out of hyperspace – right into the Imperial fleet.

From the shuttle's comlink came the voice of an Imperial controller: 'We have you on our screen now. Please identify.'

Han said, 'Shuttle *Tydirium* requesting deactivation of the deflector shield.'

Luke was suddenly filled with dread. He sensed Vader. 'I'm endangering the mission,' Luke said. 'I shouldn't have come.'

'Don't get jittery,' Han said to Luke. But he was nervous, too.

Then the controller spoke again: 'Shuttle *Tydirium*, deactivation of the shield will commence immediately. Follow your present course.'

'Okay!' Han said, glancing back at his friends. 'I told you it was gonna work. No problem.'

He flew the shuttle past the Death Star, down to the forest moon of Endor.

AFTER LANDING on the forest moon, the rebels approached a clearing. Luke saw two scout troopers on speeder bikes zooming away. If they reported the rebels, the whole mission would be a failure. So Luke and Leia jumped on another speeder bike and took off after them.

Catching up to one of them, Luke leaped to the other speeder and threw off the trooper. But the second trooper fired and hit Leia's bike. Luckily, she dove off before her bike slammed into a tree.

Another trooper attacked Luke, pushing his bike towards a huge tree. Luke dived off, but he got back up quickly and ignited his lightsaber. When the scout zoomed towards him, Luke cut off the front of his bike, which then slammed into a tree in a fiery explosion.

AN EWOK, a furry native of the forest, found Leia lying on the ground. His name was Wicket. He poked her with his spear. Princess Leia woke up and said, 'Cut it out!'

Wicket jumped back.

'I'm not gonna hurt you,' Leia said gently. 'You want something to eat?'

She removed a bit of food from her pocket and held it out to him. After sniffing it carefully, Wicket took it from Leia's hand and ate it.

'Come on,' Leia said. 'Let's get out of here.'

As they moved into the forest, Wicket tugged at Leia's arm. Figuring that her newfound friend knew his way around better than she did, Leia decided to follow him.

ON THE DEATH STAR, two guards stood watch in the Emperor's throne room. The turbolift door slid open and Darth Vader entered. The Emperor said, 'I told you to remain on the command ship.'

'A small rebel force has penetrated the shield and landed on Endor,' Vader replied. 'My son is with them. I have *felt* him, my master.'

'Strange that I have not,' the Emperor said warily. Leaning forward in his chair, he continued. 'I wonder if your feelings on this matter are clear, Lord Vader.'

'They are clear, my master.'

'Then you must go to the Sanctuary Moon and wait for him.'

Vader was sceptical. 'He will come to me?'

'I have foreseen it,' the Emperor said.

CHEWBACCA SNIFFED

at the air and growled.

'What is it, Chewie?' Han asked.

Chewbacca barked. Luke, Han, Chewie and the droids were looking for Princess Leia. The Wookiee led them to a dead animal carcass. Unable to resist, Chewbacca reached for the carcass – which triggered a trap! The next thing they knew, they were lifted high above the ground in a net. R2-D2 quickly extended a circular saw and cut through the net. They all fell to the ground. As they got up, they were surrounded by many Ewoks armed with stone-tipped spears and knives.

At the sight of C-3PO, however, they began to chant and bow down before the golden droid. They seemed to think C-3PO was some kind of god. Unfortunately, the Ewoks didn't think much of C-3PO's friends.

● ● ● ● ● ● ● ●

A PROCESSION WALKED THROUGH the dark forest with their prisoners, each of whom was tied to a long pole carried on the shoulders of Ewoks. Soon they reached a village. Leia and Wicket emerged from a large hut. Leia told the Ewoks that the prisoners were her friends and they should be set free. But the Ewoks refused.

Luke said, 'Threepio, tell them if they don't do as you wish, you'll become angry and use your magic.'

Then Luke used the Force to levitate C-3PO's throne. The Ewoks fell back in terror and released their prisoners. Later, the Ewok tribe listened in amazement to C-3PO's story of the rebels' adventures against the Empire.

The Ewok elders talked with C-3PO, who then exclaimed, 'Wonderful! We are now a part of the tribe.'

LEIA FOLLOWED LUKE OUTSIDE. She asked, 'Luke, what's wrong?'

Luke hesitated, then said, 'Vader is here ... now, on this moon. That's why I have to go. I have to face him.'

'Why?'

'He's my father.'

'Your father?' Leia gasped.

'There's more,' Luke said. 'It won't be easy for you to hear it, but you must. If I don't make it back, you're the only hope for the Alliance. The Force is strong in my family. My father has it ... I have it ...' Then he looked at Leia as he added, 'And my sister has it.'

Leia stared into Luke's eyes. 'Yes,' Luke said. 'It's you, Leia.'

'I know. Somehow ... I've always known,' she said.

Luke hugged his sister, then walked off into the forest.

THE REBEL ALLIANCE FLEET prepared for their flight to the Death Star. Lando Calrissian sat in the cockpit of the *Millennium Falcon* with his copilot, a Sullustan named Nien Nunb. Behind them, two rebel soldiers checked the *Falcon*'s navigational and shield controls.

Lando guided the *Falcon* past the larger battle cruisers. He was followed by a group of starfighters that included X-wings, A-wings, B-wings and Y-wings.

'Admiral, we're in position,' Lando reported into his comlink. The Mon Calamari Admiral Ackbar was in charge of the Death Star assault.

Admiral Ackbar's voice came from the comm: 'All groups assume attack coordinates.'

Nien Nunb was nervous, but Lando said, 'My friend's down there. He'll have that shield down on time.'

Then the entire rebel armada made the jump to hyperspace.

THE FLEET DROPPED OUT of hyperspace and the rebel ships headed straight for the Death Star. From his command cruiser, Admiral Ackbar said, 'May the Force be with us.'

In the *Falcon*'s cockpit, Nien Nunb couldn't get a reading on the Death Star's energy shield. Lando said, 'We've got to be able to get *some* kind of a reading on that shield.'

Nien Nunb responded in his alien language, and Lando said, 'Well, how could they be jamming us if they don't know we're coming?' And then Lando realised the truth: the Empire *did* know they were coming. 'Break off the attack!' he yelled. 'The shield is still up.'

The *Falcon* and the rebel starfighters all veered off to avoid crashing into the energy shield.

Admiral Ackbar said, 'It's a trap!'

THE *FALCON* and the other ships had turned straight into an armada of Star Destroyers. Then Lando saw hundreds of TIE fighters, which were targeting the rebel fleet.

'There's too many of them!' a rebel pilot shouted. A moment later, his ship was struck by enemy fire and it exploded.

Flying through the battle, Lando ordered, 'Accelerate to attack speed!'

Suddenly, an explosion rocked the rebel fleet as a cruiser was blown apart. Lando was stunned. 'That blast came from the Death Star!' he exclaimed. 'That thing's operational!'

Admiral Ackbar said, 'All craft prepare to retreat.'

'Han will have that shield down,' Lando promised. 'We've got to give him more time.'

'THIS IS A REBEL THAT
SURRENDERED TO US.
HE WAS ARMED ONLY WITH THIS.'

AS VADER'S SHUTTLE touched down on the forest moon, a walker lurched towards the landing platform. Vader disembarked and the walker's hatch slid up to reveal ... Luke Skywalker.

An officer said, 'This is a rebel that surrendered to us. He was armed only with this.'

The officer handed Luke's lightsaber over to Vader.

Vader ignited the brilliant green blade. 'Your skills are complete. Indeed, you are powerful, as the Emperor has foreseen.'

'Search your feelings, Father,' Luke said. 'I feel the conflict within you. Let go of your hate.'

'It is too late for me, Son,' Vader replied. 'The Emperor will show you the true nature of the Force. He is your master now.'

'Then my father is truly dead,' Luke said sadly.

PRINCESS LEIA, HAN SOLO, CHEWBACCA and the rebel commandos broke into the bunker containing the controls for the shield generator. They were about to blow up the bunker when they were captured by Imperials! Their Imperial captors led them outside, where they were surrounded by over a hundred Imperial troops.

C-3PO called to the stormtroopers from the nearby forest, trying to get their attention. When a group of stormtroopers approached to take C-3PO prisoner, a band of Ewoks jumped down from the surrounding trees! The Ewoks carried clubs, stones, knives and spears. Their attack was swift and ferocious, and most of the stormtroopers fell without knowing what had hit them.

Han and Chewbacca used the distraction to run back into the bunker and place several explosive charges. Then Han ran out of the bunker shouting, 'Move! Move!'

Chewbacca and the other rebels ran for cover. A moment later, the bunker and the shield generator blew up in a series of explosions.

IN THE HIGHEST TOWER of the Death Star, Darth Vader and Luke arrived in the Emperor's throne room. Vader handed Luke's lightsaber to his master.

'Welcome, young Skywalker,' the Emperor said. 'I'm looking forward to completing your training. In time you will call *me* Master.'

Luke moved fast, using the Force to call his lightsaber from where it sat on the Emperor's throne. He then engaged his father in a vicious duel. Luke drove Vader back to the stairway, beating him down.

'Good! Your hate has made you powerful,' the Emperor said, cackling. 'Now, fulfil your destiny and take your father's place at *my* side!'

Then Luke made a fateful decision. He flung aside his lightsaber and said, 'I'll never turn to the dark side. You've failed, Your Highness. I am a Jedi, like my father before me.'

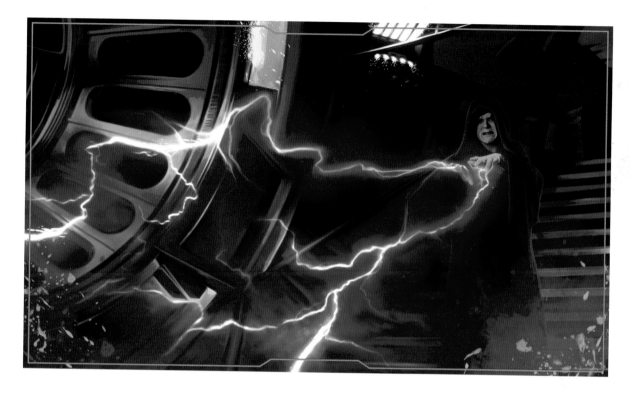

THE EMPEROR SAID, 'If you will not be turned, you will be *destroyed*.' He raised his arms and extended his gnarled fingers towards Luke. Bolts of blue lightning shot from the Emperor's hands, and Luke was enveloped by crackling bands of energy. As the lightning burned his son, Vader struggled to his feet.

'Young *fool* ... ,' the Emperor sneered, 'only now, at the end, do you understand.'

More blue lightning swept through Luke.

'Your feeble skills are no match for the *power* of the dark side,' the Emperor said.

Using the last of his strength, Luke lifted his arm and reached out towards Vader. 'Father, please,' Luke groaned. 'Help me.'

Preparing for a final deadly blast, the Emperor snarled, 'Now, young Skywalker ... you will die.'

LUKE WAS HIT by a wave of painful lightning. His screams echoed across the throne room.

Darth Vader continued to stand and watch. Then something changed. Despite all the terrible, unspeakable things he'd done in his life, he suddenly realised he could not allow the Emperor to kill his son. In that moment, he was no longer Darth Vader.

He was Anakin Skywalker.

He grabbed the Emperor from behind and hurled him into the shaft. The Emperor screamed as his he plunged into the pit. Then his body exploded, releasing dark energy and creating a rush of air up through the throne room.

Luke crawled the short distance to his father's side and pulled him away from the edge of the abyss.

ADMIRAL ACKBAR announced, 'The shield is down! Commence attack on the Death Star's main reactor.'

From the *Falcon*, Lando said, 'We're on our way!'

The *Falcon* zipped into the exhaust port with the other rebel fighters right behind. But three TIE fighters zoomed in after them – and they were quickly followed by a trio of dagger-winged TIE interceptors.

Lando adjusted a switch on his console, then said into his comlink, 'Now lock on to the strongest power source. It should be the power generator.'

As they continued to race for the reactor core, laser fire tore past them from behind. The X-wing at the rear of the group was hit, and it exploded in the tunnel.

IN A DEATH STAR HANGAR, Luke struggled to haul Darth Vader to the shuttle. Vader lay back against the ramp. From the corridor outside the hangar came the sound of more explosions.

'Luke,' Vader gasped, 'help me take this mask off.'

Slowly, Luke lifted the helmet off, and he saw his father's face for the first time.

Anakin smiled weakly and said, 'Now … go, my son. Leave me.'

'No,' Luke said. 'You're coming with me. I've got to save you.'

Anakin smiled again. 'You already have, Luke. You were right.' Choking, he gasped, 'You were right about me. Tell your sister … you were right.'

Anakin Skywalker was dead. Luke piloted the shuttle away from the Death Star.

THE FALCON FLEW into the Death Star's reactor core. Lando fired the missiles, which scored direct hits. Behind him, a TIE interceptor was vaporised. Just as the *Falcon* sped back into the tunnel, the entire reactor core was filled with superheated gases that rushed after the starships.

Behind the *Falcon*, the wave of intense heat caught up with another TIE interceptor and the ship was transformed into a fireball. A mass of jet flame blasted out from the exhaust port just as the *Falcon* broke away from the Death Star.

Lando let out a loud victory cry and the Death Star exploded. The blast was so brilliant and enormous that it could be seen from the forest moon!

DARKNESS HAD FALLEN

on the forest moon when Luke carried a flaming torch to the logs he'd stacked in a clearing. He set the torch to the logs and they began to burn. On top of the pyre lay his father's body.

Standing alone, Luke watched the fire and felt the heat of its blaze. The flames rose high into the night. Fireworks exploded overhead, and then starfighters streaked across the sky. Luke realised his allies were celebrating.

News of the Rebel Alliance victory had spread quickly across the galaxy, to Cloud City, Tatooine, Naboo and Coruscant.

When the pyre had burned out, Luke went to find his friends.

HIGH ABOVE the forest floor, a wild celebration was taking place in the Ewok village. All the rebels – even the droids – were dancing. Lando arrived and was greeted by Han and Chewbacca. Then Luke appeared, and his friends rushed to greet and embrace him.

Stepping away from the others, Luke gazed into the night and saw three shimmering apparitions: Yoda, Ben Kenobi and a younger Anakin Skywalker. Luke was right: he was a Jedi like his father before him. The apparitions smiled at Luke, silently telling him that the Force would be with him ... always.

Leia came to Luke's side and took his hand, then led him back to the others.

The celebration went on long into the night.

MAY THE FORCE BE WITH YOU!